To Maeve and Ronan
FROM
Avô

8/14/2020

SORRY, GROWN-UPS, YOU CAN'T GO TO SCHOOL!

by **Christina Geist** • illustrated by **Tim Bowers**

Random House 🏠 New York

Text copyright © 2019 by Christina Geist
Jacket art and interior illustrations copyright © 2019 by Tim Bowers

All rights reserved. Published in the United States by Random House
Children's Books, a division of Penguin Random House LLC, New York.

Random House and the colophon are registered trademarks of Penguin Random House LLC.

Visit us on the Web! rhcbooks.com

Educators and librarians, for a variety of teaching tools, visit us at RHTeachersLibrarians.com

Library of Congress Cataloging-in-Publication Data
Names: Geist, Christina, author. | Bowers, Tim, illustrator.
Title: Sorry, grown-ups, you can't go to school! / by Christina Geist ; illustrated by Tim Bowers.
Other titles: Sorry, grown-ups, you cannot go to school!
Description: First edition. | New York : Random House, [2019] |
Summary: Lady and Buddy must insist that school is only for children and teachers when their parents, grandparents,
and even a dog get excited about joining them for games, stories, and experiments.
Identifiers: LCCN 2018033279 (print) | LCCN 2018038681 (ebook) |
ISBN 978-1-5247-7086-0 (ebook) | ISBN 978-1-5247-7084-6 (hardcover) |
ISBN 978-1-5247-7085-3 (hardcover library binding)
Subjects: | CYAC: Schools—Fiction. | Parent and child—Fiction. | Grandparent and child—Fiction. | Humorous stories.
Classification: LCC PZ7.S2502 (ebook) | LCC PZ7.S2502 Sor 2019 (print) |
DDC [E]—dc23

MANUFACTURED IN THE UNITED STATES OF AMERICA
10 9 8 7 6 5 4 3
First Edition

To my parents, Joyce and Vin.
"Who's Better Than You?!"
—C.G.

To Brylie, Grady, and Caleb
—T.B.

It seemed like any other school day.
But as soon as Lady and her brother,
Buddy, were dressed and eating breakfast
at the kitchen table, things started to get
a little weird.

"Good morning!" said Mom.
"Check out my new backpack!
It has four zippers and a secret
pocket. I'm wearing it to school!"
 Sorry, Mommy.
 You can't go to school.
 Only kids and teachers.
 Only kids and teachers.

"Hey!" yelled Dad. "Look at my new high-tops! I can tie them all by myself. I'm wearing them to school!"

Sorry, Daddy.
You can't go to school.
Only kids and teachers.
Only kids and teachers.

Just then, the doorbell rang. It was
Grandma and Grandpa and Bow-wow.
And they were all wearing backpacks!

Sorry, grown-ups!
You can't go to school!
Only kids and teachers!
Only kids and teachers!

Ruff. Ruff. Ruff! barked Bow-wow.

Ru-ruff,

ru-ruff-ruff-RUFF?

SORRY, BOW-WOW!

YOU CAN'T GO TO SCHOOL!

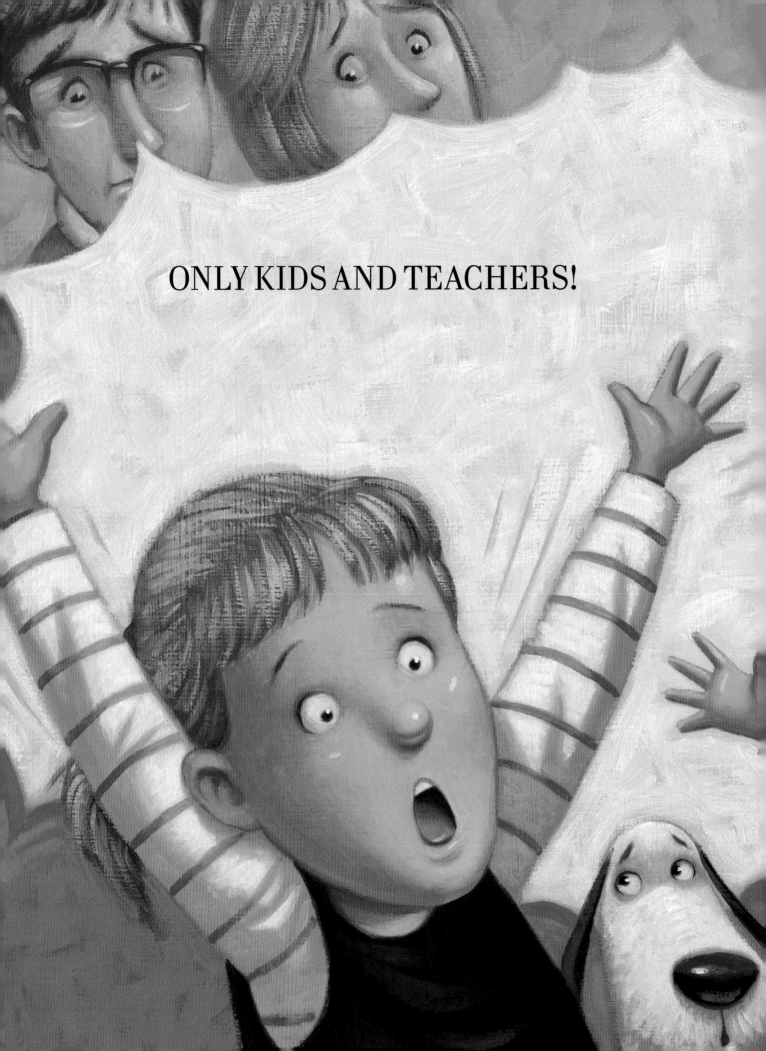

ONLY KIDS AND TEACHERS!

"IT'S NOT FAIR!" yelled the grown-ups.

"We want to go to morning meeting!"

"We want to play ABC games . . ."

"...and read stories on the cozy carpet!"

"We want to do science experiments!"

"We want to play with our friends at recess!"

"We're sorry," said Lady. "It's just the way it is."
"Yeah," said Buddy. "Some things are for you,
and some things are for us. It's just the way it is."

"But you can pick us up at the end of the day! And you can even take us to the playground on the way home!"

"And we'll tell you all about
school at family dinner tonight!"

"Don't forget—tomorrow
we get to go to work with *you*!"